WHY SPIDER SPINS TALES

Debby Pourroy

First-Start® Legends

WHY SPIDER SPINS TALES

A STORY FROM AFRICA

Retold by Janet Palazzo-Craig
Illustrated by Dave Albers

Troll

    Long ago, there lived a
Spider. He could spin
beautiful webs.

    But Spider also wanted to
spin stories. Beautiful stories,
sad stories, exciting stories!

At that time, all the stories belonged to the Sky God. Spider went to see him.

"May I have your stories?" Spider asked.

The Sky God laughed. "I will give you the stories if you bring me four things: Python, the Hornets, Leopard, and Fairy."

Spider went home. He asked his wife, "How shall I catch Python?"

"Get a branch and some vines," she said. "Bring them to Python's home."

Spider did so.

As Spider walked along, he spoke. "It *is* longer than Python," he said.

"No, it is not," he answered himself, pretending to be his wife.

"Yes, it is."

"No, it is not."

"There is Python," said Spider. "I will ask him."

Python had heard all this. He asked, "What are you talking about?"

Spider told him that he thought Python was not as long as the branch. His wife thought Python was longer.

"I will lie next to the branch to find out," said Python. As he did— *zip, zip!* Spider tied Python to the branch with the vines.

"Now I have you!" said Spider.

Happily, Spider went home. "Now I must catch the Hornets," he said.

His wife told him, "Fill a bowl with water and go to the forest."

Spider did so.

Soon he heard the buzzing Hornets. He climbed a tree. He sprinkled water on them.

Then Spider put a big leaf over his head. "Hornets," he said, "it is raining. Come keep dry in my bowl."

Buzzzzzz—into the bowl they flew. Quickly Spider put the leaf over the bowl.

"Now I have you!" he said.

 When Spider got home, he said, "Now I must catch Leopard."

"Dig a deep hole," said his wife.

Spider did so. He put branches over the hole to cover it.

The next day, Leopard was at the bottom of the hole. "Help me," he called.

Spider put two branches into the hole. "Climb up," he told Leopard.

Leopard did not see the cage at the top of the hole. He climbed up. *Thump*— the cage door slammed shut!

"I have you now," said Spider.

"I will catch Fairy next," said Spider.

He made a wooden doll and put sticky sap from the gum tree on it. He tied a string around the doll. In a bowl, he put some yams. Then he hid and waited for Fairy.

When Fairy came along, she asked the doll, "May I have some of your yams?"

Unseen, Spider pulled the string. The doll nodded.

"May I have more?" asked Fairy. This time, the doll did not move. "Speak!" said Fairy. She shook the doll. Both her hands stuck fast to the gummy sap.

"I have you!" said Spider.

   Spider went to see the Sky God. "Here are Python, the Hornets, Leopard, and Fairy. May I have your stories now?" said Spider.

"Spider," said the Sky God, "you have done what others could not. I give you my stories. We shall call them Spider Stories!"

And so it came to pass
that Spider could spin
stories. Beautiful
stories, sad stories,
exciting stories—for all
to enjoy!

Why Spider Spins Tales is all about storytelling. Spider is also the hero of several other stories told in West Africa by the Akan people. Spider is a tricky fellow. His trickiness helps him to overpower many larger animals.

A number of the Spider tales came to the New World with the slaves. In the American South, they are known as "Aunt Nancy" stories. That is because Spider's Akan name is "Ananse."